JORDAN SILVER

T-Bone Riley is a man of few words. Raised pretty much off the grid his whole life, he tends to see things a little different. Now that he's all alone after the death of his dad, he's thinking it may be time to find him some company. Seeing as he's a throwback to the old days, when he sees the little filly's ass on the campus grounds, he doesn't think there's a damn thing wrong with nabbing her and taking her back to the farm to warm his bed and bear his children.

Redneck
Jordan Silver

Now Available for Preorder
Savage

Titles by Jordan Silver

SEAL Team Series
Connor
Logan
Zak
Tyler
Cord

The Lyon Series
Lyon's Crew
Lyon's Angel
Lyon's Way
Lyon's Heart
Lyon's Family

Passion
Passion
Rebound

The Pregnancy Series
His One Sweet Thing
The Sweetest Revenge
Sweet Redemption

JORDAN SILVER

The Mancini Way
Catch Me if You Can

The Bad Girls Series
The Temptress
The Seductress

Other Titles by Jordan Silver
His Wants (A Prequel)
Taking What He Wants
Stolen
The Brit
The Homecoming
The Soccer Mom's Bad Boy
The Daughter In Law
Southern Heat
His Secret Child
Betrayed
Night Visits
The Soldier's Lady
Billionaire's Fetish
Rough Riders
Stryker
Caleb's Blessing
The Claiming
Man of Steel
Fervor
My Little Book of Erotic Tales
Tryst
His Xmas Surprise
Tease

JORDAN SILVER

Biker's Law
Bad Santa

Jordan Silver Writing as Jasmine Starr
The Purrfect Pet Series
Pet
Training His Pet
His Submissive Pet
Breeding His Pet

Jordan Siler Writing as Tiffany Lordes
American Gangster
Double The Trouble

JORDAN SILVER

locales, or persons, living or dead, is
coincidental.

Chapter 1

T-Bone

***

Most people always want to be somewhere, seeing something, being something or doing something else. Anything other than what they are right then and there. No one's content with their lot in life.... And then you have those who just don't give a fuck. Like me. Name's T-Bone!

I have a whole other way of doing things. I live by my own rules and don't give that fuck about who likes it or not. It comes from having been raised off the grid most of my life I guess. Out here where I am, it's just me and the land and whatever nature sends my way.

When you live the way I did the first half of my life, you learn to make your own rules and they mostly revolve around survival. My rules and this man's laws don't necessarily jive

together. The law tends to be a bit confused as to what's right and wrong if you ask me. And that's where we part company.

For instance, like the time I came back home to the farm early, after heading into town, and caught my fiancée and some pampered dick heating up the sheets. I didn't say nothing, didn't make no fuss. I never was one to waste my time and energy.

I just stood in that doorway watching for a minute or so before I called out, 'hey y'all.' Then pulled my gun and blew them both to kingdom come. I made sure they were done for, even a wild animal deserves to be put out of its misery after all, and without missing a beat turned right around and took myself off down to the sheriff's office.

"Sheriff, I just shot me two rabid coons in heat." That was on account of if anyone had heard those shots outside of hunting season there wouldn't be much of a fuss about it. Folks tend to stick their nose in sometimes where they not needed.

I'd headed back home to the farm and fed my hogs and that was that. Wasn't much fuss to be made in these parts since no one knew too much about the gal seeing as she was an outsider and hadn't been around all that long.

If she hadn't traipsed her ass into town that one time to lord it over the town folk with her finery they wouldn't have known she was here in the first place. But like I said, folks around here are nosy and they noticed a lot.

The story started floating around about how poor T-Bone had been done wrong. How his fancy fiancée had up and ran off with her beau. Now the thing is, most believed that, because to them I'm about the sorriest sight this side a Texas. I tend to like it that way.

I have a face full of hair, and the one on my head grows down past my shoulders. I could hardly remember what I looked like before the age of sixteen. That's because it was about then that I'd started growing that beard a

mine and covering half my face with a bandana and my eyes with some cheap Dollar General shades.

Well, the men might say all manner of things, but if they only knew what some of their women offer me with their eyes, they'd grow a beard too. But it's none of my business, and I'm all about minding my own.

Now some might say I could afford not to give a fuck because of the money, but that ain't true. I was just wired that way somehow and through life and circumstance it had only grown worse over time. Money didn't have spit to do with it. A man's mettle should never be measured by such a thing. No real man's anyhow.

I guess you'll be wanting to know how a scruffy scalawag like me came by so much money as to be able to thumb my nose at convention. Well now, that's a story in itself.

My daddy was the meanest so and so this side a Texas, come to think of it on either side. Word around town is he'd worked my

mama into the ground with backbreaking work and pure old cussedness and had started in on me as soon as I could pick my head up. Word ain't worth shit.

I was all of six or seven when my mama up and died, and daddy took me out of school to help around the farm, which wasn't much of one to begin with.

We had a few head of cattle, some hogs, and maybe a sheep or two. Not much when you think about it. What we did have; was a stud bull that bred just about every heifer in a thousand mile radius. He was mean too.

The town folk's tongues got to wagging early on-on account of how pitiful we looked whenever we were out and about. Folks tend to judge a man by his clothes or what kinda truck he drove, more so than what he had on the inside.

I used to follow my old man to town in a pair of old pants that were held up by rope because they were too big around the middle, with my ankles showing because they were too

JORDAN SILVER

short in the legs. An old ratty shirt with the sleeves gnawed off by a hound dog and an old straw hat that was more straw than hat.

Some folks use to say that the old man used to be a right good looking feller in his younger days. How my daddy used to get to hooting and hollering, and raising hell.

That was before the cares of the world beat him down and he just about gave up on life, except for his wife and son. Folks used to whisper that I was shaping up to be just like 'im.

I didn't talk much, not then and not now, so folks got to minding our business. Once they'd even got the county to send a social worker out to our place.

In the end them folks couldn't figure how the old man was such an abuser since there was never a scratch on me and I looked up to him something fierce.

Sure he'd taken me outta school to help out, but I'd taken myself down to the schooling

place and signed me up for homeschooling. The busybodies in town didn't know that. Then again there was a lot they didn't know.

My daddy, he wasn't much for talking either. He spoke in spit, grunts and 'git it boy.' That last was to a mean old dog he had around the place that he'd sic on anything with two feet and a heartbeat.

He used to sic 'im on me too. That dog would run my poor ass up a tree every time, until I turned him to my side. I'd feed him scraps when daddy wasn't looking and after that there was no more fun for the old man.

Then one day the old bull up and kicked daddy in the balls. He probably decided there was only room for one stud on the farm and he was it. The two of them sure did have an ornery relationship.

So now daddy from that day was always just fair to middling and I was the one left to keep the place up. It was back breaking work to be sure, but I wouldn't have had it any other way. I got to enjoy the outdoors as much as I

like, and do as I please even down to swimming
bare assed naked down by the creek.

Chapter 2

T-Bone

***

Now how we come by all this money. The Rileys, that's our last name, were land rich and dirt poor for as long as anyone could remember. Old Silas, my daddy, had inherited the land from his daddy and his daddy from his and so on and so forth going back a couple hundred years.

There wasn't never much of nothing good coming from it, until that day I went to walking to get away from daddy's misery. I'd just turned eighteen and my days were spent taking care of the animals and him. Scared that I was gonna lose him just like I'd lost mama and be all-alone.

I didn't mind being alone so much it's what I was used to. But if daddy died then I wouldn't have nobody on this earth, nary a soul. I hadn't given it much thought until now

and that's what got me to walking the land lost in my own head.

I could go into town and make me a few friends I guess. There was always somebody trying to talk to me wherever I went. But I wasn't too fond of city ways and wasn't much interested in them coming out here neither.

So there I was walking the land and thinking about what was to become of me. I was throwing a stick for that old dog to catch not really paying too much mind when it happened. The stick landed in the brush somewheres and that poor dog got to whining something awful until I went and got it out.

That's when I found it. Texas gold. The darkest purest oil anyone had seen in these parts in some time. I knew what it was right then and there but it didn't mean much to me. Like all the men of my family before me, I was very content with my life as it was.

Not that money wouldn't be nice. But it wasn't as good as having daddy back on his feet and healthy.

Well, the money started coming in after that, and anyone who thought they could get over on me had another think coming. I was smarter than most folks gave me credit for.

I'd taken to that schooling well enough on my own and knew what was what. No accountants and lawyers for me. I figured the old timers didn't need one and neither did I.

I took to reading anything I could get my hands on to help me wade through the muck and mire of the money grubbers who all came calling with their hands out. Thing is, I mostly read the stuff one of my great grandfathers had left behind. It worked then I don't see why it can't work now. Far as I know nobody changed them laws in over two hundred years.

Well after the oil made us rich as Croesus, daddy up and died from his swollen ball predicament leaving me a very rich but lonely man. That's where the fiancée came in.

Now most folks thought I was simple minded on account of I never had more than my home schooling and stayed mostly to

myself not really having any friends or anyone to talk to.

So some shyster with a little less money than me but what he considered better pedigree decided he could keep his family coffers full by marrying off his daughter to the redneck simpleton. People ought not to judge a book by its cover.

I hadn't been in love with the trollop, not that she wasn't pretty enough, she was. But I'd gone along with it even though I knew what the man was up to.

I figured it was about time at twenty-six to settle down and have me a kid or two to help run the place anyway. She was pretty enough to look at so it wouldn't be a chore to bed her, and I'd have me a body to share the nights with at least.

But I don't cotton to being betrayed. It's one thing that she was after my money, but to bring her lover in my home, the home that has been in my family for generations, was a slight I cannot and will not forgive.

After I'd shot her and the adulterer and fed them to my hogs, I'd gone off and bought all the surrounding land because I was plum tired of people. I was mad as spit to tell the truth and anyone who'd come nosing around my place back then wouldn't have made it off.

So to keep the peace and leave the population alive a little longer than they deserved, I'd bought out everyone around. I tore down homes, buildings and whatever else was in my way, until there was nothing left but the old log cabin that had been sitting on the land for well nigh two hundred years. My home.

The gal that was supposed to be my wife hadn't been too pleased with the living arrangements but she'd convinced herself that she could talk me into building her the biggest mansion in the state on account of she was so pretty and all.

There was never any chance in hell of that happening. I was born and raised in that cabin and I aim to die the same. I see now that

she never would've fit in around here and truth is I don't think anyone would.

Now I have four hundred thousand acres of wide-open space all to myself. I wasn't lonely so much as I was tired of my own damn company. All that was left for me to do of an evening after the work was done was to walk or ride that land.

Then one day, I was off walking by my lonesome and I got a feeling. I went to digging on account of that feeling and wouldn't you know it, there was oil right there where the Piggly Wiggly once stood.

The money kept rolling in but I was starting to get lonesome. I'd hired some hotshot to come out and teach me how to use the computer so I could do my business more efficiently and now it took me less than an hour in the mornings to look over everything.

Now that was a story in itself. That feller was just like everybody else. He took one look at me and saw a redneck with nary a lick a sense and figured he could take advantage. I

played along like I was empty between the ears, all the while learning all I needed, or all he knew anyways.

Then one day, I caught him trying to get into my personal files and the night before I'd found the doohickey he'd put on my computer so he could track everything I did and I got to shooting again. Yes sir, I hauled off and shot him in the ass.

After he had ran screaming to his car and hightailed it outta here, I took myself down to the bookstore and bought out every book they had on the subject of computers and taught myself what I needed to know. Now I can take one of them fool things apart and put it back together.

But now I'm bored and riding my ATV over the land hell bent for leather was no longer enough. At night, I'd lay in that big old four-poster bed that one of my great grandma's had bought and wish for somebody to talk to. It reminded me of the one I'd seen once in one of daddy's old funny books. The ones with all the naked women in them.

I'd lie in that big old bed and wish I had a body next to me. I needed to get started on them babies, but no matter how I thought, I couldn't come up with the answer.

I could maybe do like the folks back in my great-great-grandpa's days did and order one. But I didn't like the looks of them girls they had in them magazines. Not the one of them looked like they knew the backend of a cow.

Chapter 3

T-Bone

***

I could always head into town and get me some company, but I was tired of that, and besides none of them girls were right for what I needed. They weren't exactly the kind of girl mama would've appreciated sitting at her table come Sunday lunch.

I was thinking too that maybe I ought to do something about my education. I do have an awful hungering for learning. But all the books and what not I found on the internet wasn't the same as being in school the way I remembered.

I figured now with my daddy gone there was nothing stopping me from going out into the world and getting an education. I could maybe learn about all those places I'd seen on the Internet. Who knows, maybe one day I might even take a trip.

So I got the bright idea to go down to the college and sign up for classes, and that's when it happened.

It was my very first day on campus. I was headed to the registrar's office to sign up when I saw the raven-haired angel. Her hair fell straight as a pin to the top of her ass.

I didn't see much more than that since she was heading in the opposite direction, but I decided then and there that I wasn't letting her out of my sight. There was something about her, something that pulled at me even as I followed her from a distance. Like maybe I knew her.

She was a little bitty thing I noticed as I walked behind her, and something in my chest came alive. I don't rightly know what was going on with me, having never had that strong a reaction to anyone before, but I knew that there was something to it.

Why just looking at her made me want to just grab her up and take her home and protect her she was so little. The thought

entered my mind that maybe I wouldn't mind seeing her little belly swollen with my child either. I'm telling you the attraction I felt for her ass as it moved from side to side as I walked along behind her was awful fierce.

I bet this is how the men back in the day felt when they saw the little filly they wanted to share their bed. I'd read that way back when before men lost their damn minds and their balls, they would just grab whichever woman caught their fancy and take her home.

I've always liked that idea. And since the one time I tried doing things the way folks call civilized had ended with murder, I'm thinking I might be on to something.

She ducked into a class that was just about to get started and I followed right on her heels. It was almost as if she'd mesmerized me. I never took my eyes off her hair or that fine ass.

I measured her hips in my head and damn if she wasn't built right to carry my sons. She wasn't spread too wide and the split

between her thighs was still kinda close but I didn't mind. After I fucked her a good dozen times that should open her right up.

Anyone watching would've probably found something wrong with the strange man and the way he seemed to have the young girl in his sights as he followed behind her, not to mention the bulge in his jeans that he wasn't even trying to hide. Everybody had a suspicious mind these days.

She went to the very back of the room and I followed suit, taking the seat just behind her. I wasn't sure exactly what it was I was going to do next. I hadn't exactly planned for this circumstance. But I figured I would at least learn her name and then go from there.

You see the truth is, I don't know much about courting women. Sure daddy had taken me on my sixteenth birthday down to the playhouse to lose my virginity. And I've been back a time or two...or ten since then because after all I'm a normal red blooded male with a healthy appetite for pussy.

But other than the one I'd had to shoot, I hadn't ever been with a nice girl. Come to think of it I don't necessarily consider my ex-fiancée to be much different to the ones I've paid over the years.

Like most things, I've done my fair share of studying up on the subject and know well enough how to give a woman pleasure. I figure that stuff comes from within you one way or the other. If you love someone it ought to just come natural.

From what little I remember of mama as a young'un, she was always happy and singing in the mornings, and daddy was always petting her or making eyes at her when they thought I wasn't looking.

And since I was getting most of what I know from them books daddy had left behind, I figure I couldn't go wrong. All I needed was the right girl and this little Angel might just be it. She sure has caught my attention that's for sure.

But I didn't know the first thing about approaching a woman. One thing I do know, no more arranged marriage for me. This time I'm gonna do the picking and a choosing and ain't it grand that my first time out I found me a gem.

I'd known all along what that girl and her daddy had been up to, but I hadn't cared much one way or the other as long as I got a couple boys outta the deal.

After that fiasco however I'd been thinking I ought to maybe go about this marriage deal another way. I just never knew where to start...until today.

Now here I am sitting in this room with my mind going in ten directions at once. She sure smelt good too and that hair alone was enough to make me give up half my earthly goods. I clenched my fists so that I didn't jump the gun and reach out and touch it. That might not be considered civilized.

Most of the naked women in the old books I'd found in my parents' room after

daddy passed away had hair like that. Most of them were also naked with their pussies on display, but what the hell. The hair added a little something to the package I think. Feminine.

I felt the first stirrings of lust hit me in the gut as I imagined that hair trailing over my hot flesh as we fucked. She'd make a pretty sight riding my cock in the moonlight that comes through the bedroom window at night.

I stared at her for a good while from behind my shades before the professor came in and called the class to order. I had a story ready in case anyone asked me what the green hell I was doing here, but I just needed enough time to catch her name.

This wasn't like when I was in school as a young boy where they took attendance, so it looked like I'll have to find another way. I was sitting there staring a hole in the back of her head when she turned her blue-blue eyes back on me.

Time stood still. She was the most beautiful thing I'd ever seen in my life, and though I knew this wasn't the way things were done anymore, in that moment I made up my mind I was going to have her no matter what.

I felt the clutch in my heart right then and there and when she gave me a sweet little smile she just about sealed her fate. Some might say I have what you may call a one-track mind. I don't much think like modern folks and again this is where the 'don't give a fuck' factor comes in.

I know I'm different. I know I'd rather do things the way the men and women who settled this land preferred. And it wasn't because I was raised away from folk neither.

Well maybe that had a little something to do with it. But I know sure as spit that what I am, is what's inside of me. It's not something a man can learn, it's just who he is. I've read enough over the years to know that I maybe just a tad bit different but so what.

I think my way is better than all the foolishness men and women put themselves through these days. Time was there was no such thing as divorce. That's back when men were men and not dainty little fuckers like the one I'd had to shoot in my old bed, or the other thieving asshole I'd ran off with a shot in his ass.

I sat there as the class came to order figuring in my mind just how I was gonna get her back on the farm with me. It was gonna take some work I'm sure, but nothing I couldn't handle. My cock was already stiffening in my jeans at the thought, but I had to caution myself not to give myself away.

Thankfully, no one was paying me much mind. Everyone was too busy talking to their friend next to them or looking through their books in preparation for class. I didn't want to be here too long, not now that I had a plan in my head. It wouldn't do for too many folks to see me hanging around.

When the teacher passed out some test papers I got my chance. Peeping over her

shoulder I got what I needed. Melanie Dewitt. The name didn't sound familiar, I'd never heard the name in town before. I'm thinking that maybe for the best.

I knew how to find her now. I've been playing around on my computer enough to know you could find just about anything you wanted to right from the safety of your own home.

I got up and left the room without a word and instead of the registrar's office headed for home and my computer. I made sure to keep my head down as I walked to my truck.

No one knew what I looked like for sure, and the place was far enough away from home that if anyone did remember seeing me they might not put two and two together but still, I wasn't taking any chances.

By the time I made it back to my truck I already had a plan formed in my head. I had to get home and get things ready, but by hook or

by crook T-Bone Riley is gonna make that little beauty the mother of his children yes sir.

Chapter 4

T-Bone

***

It wasn't hard at all finding what I needed. I just pulled up the school online, looked through some pictures of the student body, and became disappointed when she wasn't there.

I wasn't discouraged for long though. After grabbing some lunch which could be better, I put her name in one of them social media things and there she was. My heart felt the same as it did in that classroom.

I stared at her picture for a good long while and let that warm feeling envelop me again. Yep, I was sure I was on the right track. That feeling never set me wrong. Every time I've had this feeling something good had come of it. As far as I'm concerned, that's all the proof I need that I am doing the right thing.

I settled down and prepared to learn all there was to know about the woman I had

chosen to be the mother of my children. I didn't let a little thing like conscience play any part in what I was planning. When a thing was right it was right no matter how you brought it about.

She was two months shy of nineteen, which as far as I was concerned was perfect. She couldn't have done much living yet. Not like some of the things I'd seen go past my computer screen. What in the green hell had the world comc to anyway?

It didn't matter anyway, for what I had in mind she'd do just fine. The fact that every time I looked at her in one of the pictures she had online I wanted to jerk my cock, only solidified things for me. I'll have to see about getting her some decent clothes though. The stuff she wears tend to look like whoever made them ran out of cloth.

I spent the rest of the day reading her social media pages until I got a good sense of what's what. She wasn't from around here, which was good. She had a mama back home in Toledo, but from what little I gathered she

wasn't much of a one so I put that worry out of my mind. The less people missing her when the time comes the better.

I was sure there would be a search at some point, but no one would think to come my way and that's all I cared about for now. It wasn't that hard to find out the particulars about where she lived in the little college town.

People ought not be so free with information like that. But it worked in my favor so what do I care? Still I'm gonna have to teach her about the dangers of broadcasting her business to the known world. Nothing good could come of that.

Next I set about getting the place ready for company. I didn't really care that I was about to become everything people had whispered about me over the years. I know me living out here on my own looking like old Grizzly Adams, scaring everyone off; people tend to get notions about a feller like that. So what?

I wasn't anything like they thought, but I wasn't much interested in proving myself to them one way or the other so it was a moot point. Truth is I knew quite a lot about those civilized citizens in town and wouldn't wish to be like nary a one of 'em.

Who wasn't sleeping with their neighbor's sweetheart, was robbing their friends and so forth. No wonder daddy always warned me to steer clear. If the way they did things was the acceptable way, then no thank you. I'll just do things the way that seem best to me and be the happier for it.

I nailed down the windows in the bedroom where I figured she'd be spending most of her time in the beginning. Next, I put a new lock on the outside of the bedroom door and one on the front and back doors as well just in case.

When I was done with the house, I went out to the barn and cut me some rope, whistling all the while. All in all it was a good deal. I'd already found a bride, and made her home ready. All that was left was to go get her.

That night, I sat down and worked out a plan of action. It was like a game to me, my own mating ritual if you will. Only I knew what I was after but that was okay.

I was sure that in the end my angel would fall in line. I wasn't planning to mistreat her after all, but to treat her the way all women ought to be.

I knew because my daddy had told me long ago that it was a woman's place to give her man as many children as her body could hold, just as it was a man's place to provide for his family, and not just food and shelter, but love. I figure I was halfway there already. If the way she stays on my mind is anything to go by anyhow.

I figured since I had the means to take care of her, the girl would be happy with her plight before long. In most of her social media posts she was always complaining about life. I figure my kid in her belly would give her something to focus on.

Out here she wouldn't have much to worry about because there won't be anyone around to bother her or stress her as she puts it. All she'd have to do for the rest of her days is raise my babies and keep me company; no stress in that.

I plan to treat her well so she would have all the love she could ever need, and with me she wouldn't have to worry about cheating and such like she and her girlfriends be talking about on that Facebook.

Chapter 5

Melanie

***

I'm not sure but I could swear someone is following me. I've had this strange feeling for the past few weeks, but every time I look around there's never anyone there. Still I couldn't shake the feeling that I was being watched.

I probably should've said something to someone, but I felt silly since I had no proof. That night I came back to the dorm from my job at the diner where I'd walked my feet into the ground, and not for the first time wished I could be like one of those trust fund babies whose daddies had deep pockets.

I knew getting an education was the only way to break the cycle of trailer trash teenage motherhood that was prevalent where I came from, but some days I wished things could be easier.

I wish I could just concentrate on school and not have to worry about anything else, but my scholarship didn't cover much more than my classes and the room I shared with my roommate. I still had to feed and clothe myself.

Mom was no help; all her money was spent on booze and whatever no good man she was shacking up with at the moment. I fumed silently as I took my shower before bed.

I turned out the lights and fell into sleep the way I always do after a long night slinging hash and grits. I don't know how much time had gone by, how long I was out before I felt something or someone in the room with me.

Somehow, I knew it wasn't my roommate because of the way the person seemed to stay in the shadows. Great, the one night she was away. I kept my eyes closed as sudden fear overtook me. I wanted to jump off the bed and run but my limbs refused to work.

I sensed movement coming from the corner and squeezed my eyes shut tighter. He was coming closer. I don't know how I knew it

was a male, but who else would sneak into my room in the middle of the damn night?

When I felt as if the intruder was leaning over me in the little twin bed, I willed myself not to open my eyes. I knew if he knew I was awake that might only make things worse. I remained still, my body tense as I awaited his next move.

I felt his hand gently brush the hair at my temple and held my breath. "Soon Angel." I think that's what the dark shadow said. What did he mean? I stupidly opened my eyes when the hand on my brow went away, but by the time they adjusted to the dark whoever he was- was gone.

I put it down to my overactive imagination or tried to, but somehow I wasn't convinced. It could be that I was so tired my mind was playing tricks on me. I mean who in their right mind would sneak into my room? I didn't know anyone here, hadn't had time between school and work to form any friendships.

By the next morning, I put the whole thing out of my mind and went on with my life.

***

T-Bone

***

I've kept myself busy gathering all the personal information I could on my angel. I went through her garbage, followed her to and from work, and in the daytime while she was in class I read up on all I'd need to take care of a nurturing mother to be.

After that one night when I'd slipped into her room and had almost been caught, I'd satisfied myself with watching her from afar. The little chart I'd started keeping after finding the tampons in her trash told me all I needed to know about her breeding season, and I knew down to the day when I would snatch her and bring her home.

As the day drew near, I grew more and more excited at the change my life was about to take. I didn't let myself think of what could go

wrong, and in the end I decided to take her one day early just in case something did go amiss.

I'd held myself back from jacking off to the pictures I'd snapped of her that night when I'd broken into her apartment, four days ago. I wanted my seed to be potent so that she'd catch on the first try. I was already born by the time daddy was my age and mama wasn't much older than she is now.

Besides if I wanted to have as many kids as I planned on it was best she get started now. I didn't want her body to wear out and all the books said she should be done having kids by the age of thirty. That gave us eleven years. I figure six kids in that amount of time was just fine.

With everything ready, three hours before it was time to go fetch my woman, I cleaned myself up before heading into town to stock up on some things. Pregnant women needed healthy food, not the can crap I usually fed myself. I hadn't gone shopping sooner because I wanted the stuff to be as close to fresh as possible.

The people in the store sure did have a lot of interest in what went into my cart but I didn't pay them no never mind. I got all the fresh fruit and vegetables I could find as well as some Angus steaks, some fresh salmon and plenty eggs.

I had plenty fresh milk on the farm. I planned to slaughter a cow sometime next week since winter was coming on. I'd had too much to do to get things ready to bring her home so that's why I hadn't done it already. I didn't think a city girl like her would cotton too much to the deer meat I had in the freezer.

I perused the aisles reading boxes to see what's what before throwing it in the cart. When I reached the register the woman behind the machine was doing her best to see behind my shades.

With all the money I had you'd think I'd have traded up by now, but I figured if it ain't broke don't fix it.

"Well T-Bone, you having outta town guests?" Well aren't you the nosy one?

"No." That wasn't the kinda no that invited more questions and she got the message right quick and buttoned her lip.

She didn't take offense, everybody know I ain't much for socializing. But there was sure to be a lot of fodder for the old gossip mill, come tomorrow.

I ain't never spent that much money on vittles before. I was more of a canned beans and luncheon meat kinda man, and here I was buying out the store of all the best meat and such.

Hopefully, she and whoever she blabbed to didn't make too much of it. I knew for sure they wouldn't dare trespass on my land to find out because they knew my gun was always at the ready.

I pushed the cart out to my old truck and loaded up before heading back to the farm. My heart didn't even skip a beat at what I was about to do. I don't see a damn thing wrong with it. As far as I'm concerned I have only the best intentions.

I was sure there might be some struggling on her part in the beginning but I'd wear her down yet. It might take a couple years at that, but by then I'd have me a couple little ones with my name, which is all I'm after.

After once again making sure everything was in place, I set out to capture my mate, and bring her home. I'd pieced together her routine from following her and from the things she'd posted online and congratulated myself on being the one to save her from certain disaster.

The way she was going, putting all her business out there for just anyone to see, it was a wonder some ill intentioned asshole hadn't snatched her already and done who knows what.

You see I don't see any correlation between that phantom someone and myself. Though I didn't do much talking, I do a lot of thinking. In my mind the end justifies the means. I know what my plans are.

That I'll be good to her and whatever children we have. I wasn't just after sex after

all, though I'll maybe fuck her all day everyday for the first month or so. But after I get her with child I don't see why we can't settle down to a fine life.

That harlot that had been in my bed said something about my antisocial tendencies once. Whatever the green hell that means.

According to her, because daddy had kept me here on the farm away from the outside world my mindset was a throwback to the old ways. And since I got everything I learned about life from the old publications daddy had kept around, I tend to be stuck in the past.

She might be right, this had a lot to do with my tendency to not give a fuck. I'm pretty sure the men and women who formed this land hadn't either.

I had a list of things I needed to pick up that I thought it best not to get in my neck of the woods, so I'd looked up some pharmacies on the way between the farm and the college.

If anyone thought it strange that a man was buying up folic acid and fertility suppositories they didn't mention it. I left the place loaded down with bags and ignored the appreciative stares from the women I passed on the way out.

I'm not that green that I didn't know women found me attractive. Some of the folks in town couldn't see past the beard and long hair. Others, especially of the female persuasion certainly did on occasion compliment me. That's why I never go anywhere without my shades.

I had one jezebel proposition me right there in the canned foods aisle of the Piggly Wiggly before I had it torn down. Told me just what she was gonna do to me, balls and all.

I heard one of the two I'd just passed whispering to the other as they went by me. 'Did you see those muscles? I bet he could go all night and then some.'

'I like the way he looked at me from behind those shades without uttering a word,

makes my heart get to fluttering. I'm gonna have me some sweet dreams tonight, just from that one look.'

What in the blue hell? They weren't even trying to be quiet. I looked around at them and they cackled like two demented hens while staring at my dick.

That's what's wrong with the world. They don't know me or what kinda man I am all they see is the few muscles I'd gotten over the years from working on the farm.

I don't put much stock in such things as looks, well not my own anyway. Angel was a beauty, but that's not to say that I couldn't have fallen for someone less attractive. Her ass just happened to be the one with my name on it is all.

I'm more interested in the kind of man I am inside. Daddy always said that a man's mettle was measured by his deeds. Like the charities I donate to all over the world that no one knew about. Or the way I cried over that old hound dog after he'd died.

I'd even had the repairs done on the old elementary school after a tornado hit and the mayor had dragged his feet. But the town folk had no idea that I was behind that and a whole lot more, because I didn't want them in my damn face with their shit. As far as I'm concerned those things, more so than all the zeroes in my bank account is what matters.

The more brazen of the two gave me a look hot enough to scorch and bit her fingertip. What the hell? "Has anyone ever told you that you look a lot like that guy in that TV show? What's his name again? She turned to her friend who was looking at me like we knew each other. I was almost afraid to open the truck for fear they might try to grab me while my back was turned. For shame!

"Jaxx, I don't remember his real name but you look a lot like him." They got to giggling again and I jumped in the truck and got the hell outta there.

Chapter 6

T-Bone

***

As I drove along on my way to my little mission, I got to thinking about those women and their reactions. You see I know I'm not what people think, though I don't try to dissuade them from their way of thinking.

I never was the ignorant hick I pretend to be, and it wasn't because of the money. Mama had been a real beauty, a woman of great taste, with a good head on her shoulders, and she'd loved daddy something fierce before she died.

They'd met at a horse show way back when daddy was doing the Rodeo circuit and daddy had brought her home and married her when he found out she was on the run from an abusive ex.

She'd given up her city life to settle down here in the middle of nowhere to have a family. Because they'd kept mostly to

themselves, people came to their own conclusions, all of them wrong.

I knew all about the finer things in life. What mama hadn't taught me I'd learned from books and now the Internet. I also knew that with my money I could go anywhere in the world, be anything I wanted. I just didn't have any interest. The land was in my blood.

All I want is to live out my days right here on this little piece of heaven with a family of my own. And for that I've decided that I need Ms. Melanie Dewitt to make it happen. She was the only woman to ever make me feel and I knew that counted for something. One day, she'll be making eyes at me the way mama had with daddy.

I pulled up outside the correct building with a few minutes to spare and after locating her car, parked just one car over. When it was just about time for her to come out, I rode around the lot slowly as if searching for a parking space.

Barring an emergency the coast should be clear. I'd chosen to move now because she should be leaving any minute for her job at the all night diner outside of town. It meant I wouldn't have to go inside and risk being seen.

My pulse picked up when I saw her come out the door with her head buried in her bag probably looking for her keys. "Oh baby that's dangerous, you should always be aware of your surroundings."

I watched her walk to her car in the poorly lit lot and eased my truck into place. There wasn't a lot of light back there and the place was empty except for the two of us. I opened the truck door as quietly as I could and snuck up behind her.

She turned just as I reached her but it was too late. There was barely a sound as she went out from the slight pressure on the pulse point in her neck. I'd thought of using the chloroform I kept around the farm, but decided against it in the end.

I made short work of tying her up once I had her safely in the truck. I knew I couldn't hang around there too long, so I just threw the sack over her head. I made sure she could breathe okay, before pulling out with her head resting on my leg. I was whistling by the time I turned the corner.

***

I rode well within the limits until I reached the far end of my property. I let himself relax as soon as the tires hit the dirt road that ran along the back of my place. She started making waking noises so I took the sack from over her head.

"Hello Angel." She screeched and tried moving off my leg but her bound hands and feet had her a bit encumbered. "Stop that before you hurt yourself." Her eyes turned up to mine and I saw the question in her eyes seconds before recognition hit.

"Why?" It was all she said as the fear clouded her eyes. I didn't like seeing it there,

but knew it would take time before she understood.
 "Why not?"

We drove on in silence partly because I refused to answer any questions and I'm sure she wasn't saying much because she was doing her best to come up with a plan of escape. It's what I would do. But there was no way out for her.

***

Melanie

***

I remember where I'd seen him before, that day in class. It was hard to miss the man with the hairy face and ponytail. Now all the times I'd felt as if I were being watched made sense.

I sat as close to the passenger door as possible once the strange man helped me sit up, but with my hands and feet tied I knew it would be pointless to try anything. I'd have to

keep my eyes and ears opened for my first chance.

My heart was pounding in my chest and my mouth was dry. Had he been the one in my room that night? The one who'd whispered 'soon'?

I eyed him out the side of my eye, sizing him up. The size of him put fear in my heart. I knew if it came down to a fight between the two of us I'd lose for sure. He was big, much bigger than my five-two, maybe six-four would be my guess.

His wrists on the steering wheel were big around, but I could tell from the fit of his clothes that he wasn't fat, not at all. His arms filled out the old western shirt he wore and his thighs looked well formed beneath his jeans.

It was his face that scared me most. That gruff mountain man look. I couldn't even see his features behind all that hair, and his shades covered his eyes.

Looking around at my surroundings didn't give me much hope. It had been a while since I'd seen anything resembling a landmark. All that was out there as far as the eye could see was vast open space, with a backdrop of tall trees.

The window was up and there was no sound inside the truck as it moved over the rugged land. I felt my tummy drop and real fear kicked in when I saw the structure up ahead what felt like hours later. My survival instinct kicked in and I made a grab for the door handle and tried to jump out.

A hand in my hair pulling me back in stopped me. I yelped from the sting and his hold eased immediately.

"Ouch." I lifted my bound hands to his wrist and tried to get him to let go altogether. "You'll hurt yourself Melanie Angel, just wait until I come around and get your door for you."

Was he insane? He was talking like we were out on a date. The question made bile rise in my throat as the reality of my situation

kicked in. Was he insane? What was he planning to do to me?

We were in the middle of nowhere. I had no concept of how long we'd been driving but I knew it was more than an hour. How would anyone find me?

I tried to remember if I'd left my car door open, if I'd left anything back there to tip someone off that I was in trouble. Maybe I'd dropped some stuff near my car door. Obviously anyone seeing that would put two and two together.

When I saw my bag on the floor between his feet my heart sank. If I'd left it back there at least that would've been evidence that something was wrong.

But this way people might think I'd just ran off or something and who knows how long it would be before they came looking. The tears started as soon as he turned the ignition off and opened his door.

Chapter 7

T-Bone

***

I heard the soft whimpers as I turned the key and hardened myself against them. I'd already resolved myself to the fact that it was gonna take work to get the little filly to see things my way.

I'd read daddy's old periodicals from the eighteen hundreds enough to know how this works. First she'd put up a fuss and so on, but as time went on she'd come to accept her lot.

There was no other outcome as far as I'm concerned, since there was no turning back. I couldn't very well take her back now could I? Not that I'd even consider it.

I'm not a complete ass. I knew damn well the world didn't work that way, that what I was doing might be considered...illegal. I just don't give a fuck.

I climbed out of the truck and walked around to her side. For the first time since my youth I felt real excitement at taking a woman. My cock was already making a tent in my jeans and I ran my hand over it to keep it calm.

I knew I was well proportioned because the women down at the playhouse had cooed over my dick every time, and even that Jezebel I'd dispatched to hell had had a fine time riding it when I'd let her.

I didn't want to think about her now however, or the others, because it felt like a betrayal of my Angel, so I put those thoughts aside.

I opened the door and reached in for her and her feet came up. My reflexes were good enough that I turned and caught the blow to my side instead of my balls, which seemed to be what she was aiming for.

A hard smack to her ass quieted her down some, but only for a second or two. She screamed bloody murder and struggled something fierce and I was glad of the fact that

I'd bought out all the land around or she would've for sure alerted my nosy ass neighbors.

"Shh, little Angel, no need to make a fuss." I was as gentle as I could be as I bundled her into my arms. That scent of hers, like honeysuckle, was playing hell with my senses.

The moon and stars were the only light this far out. No street lights, no porch lights from neighboring houses. It was just the two of us and the nocturnal critters.

I didn't have a plan worked out other than getting her bred, so I was playing it by ear. Right now the excitement of the situation had my blood up and I wanted to fuck.

I took her inside and laid her across the bed I'd prepared for her homecoming.
"Are you going to kill me?" Her words stopped me in my tracks and almost knocked me off my feet. "No." The thought never entered my head. Why would she even think such a thing?

Her eyes followed me around the room as I moved about. When I turned back to her with the knife in my hand she started kicking her legs as she screamed to be let go.

I figured there was no use trying to convince her that I wasn't gonna hurt her with the thing so I just went about cutting away her clothes. I then took her bound hands and cut the rope I'd used to tie her up before pulling her arms above her head.

I secured them to each post making sure they were tight but not cutting into her skin. With that done, I moved onto her legs and did the same. I was very patient with her as she struggled against me, only spanking her legs once or twice with a gruff 'quit it Angel'.

When I was finished, I looked down at my handy work. She was a pretty sight that's for sure. Her young nubile body spread out for my pleasure. She had a nice patch of black curls covering her pussy and her tits were nice and firm with pretty little pink tips.

Pretty soon they'd be filled with the milk needed to feed my babies. The thought made my ten-inch cock grow a little harder.

I have a very clear picture in my head of how I wanted things to go, and again not having much experience with the outside world, I'd read up on what a man in my position would have to do to get there.

You'd be surprised at what you can learn on the internet, and I'd learned plenty. I'd left no stone unturned.

I'd made up a batch of special lemonade and ground up some pain pills I use for the horses that was sure to knock her out for a spell. I left the room and came back with a thermos full.

"I want you to drink this, it'll make you feel better."
"What is it?" She stared at the flask suspiciously as I approached the bed and tried in vain to get away when I sat next to her.

"Nothing to fear you, I promise." I had to hold her head up and force her mouth open to get her to behave, but again I was as patient as could be with my little baby mama.

I fed her the concoction until the thermos was empty; then putting it aside I brushed her beautiful hair with my fingers. "You see, nothing to worry about." I kissed her head to let her know in some small way that her life wasn't in danger.

"I feel..." that was as far as she got before her eyes drooped and her neck rolled to the side on my arm, scaring me half to death. Had I given her too much?

I laid her back on the bed and checked her pulse and her breathing just the way I used to with daddy, and finding all to be as it should, breathed easy again. "I'm sorry sweet Angel."

I studied her as I got up to remove my shirt. There was no movement so I shed my jeans and underwear, standing next to the bed with my ten-inch monster at the ready.

JORDAN SILVER

I got the bag from the pharmacy and opened one of the bullet shaped tablets. I slipped it into her ass and pushed it in as far as my finger could reach.

Once that was done I cleaned my hands up in the bathroom and went back to the bed, just standing there watching her. I'd done it. After tonight I won't ever be lonesome again. My dick was so hard it hurt.

Stroking myself, I climbed onto the bed between her spread legs. I reached out to touch the soft white skin of her inner thigh gently. My heart was near to bursting, as I got closer to her pussy. I couldn't resist the urge to inhale her scent, so laying myself flat between her thighs I used both hands to open her up.

I sniffed her scent and my cock jumped, 'ummmmmm', but nothing compared to when I put my tongue in her. That taste. I love to eat pussy, but there had never been one this good, because she was all mine.

I spread her open the way the book had said, searching for her innocence, and my chest

swelled with pride when I saw that little bit of pink flesh deep inside her.

My little Angel was pure. She's my first virgin. And if I have anything to say about it, my last. My mind was filled with the knowledge that she would be the last woman I lay with.

I fingered her pussy, going only as far as her hymen while teasing her clit with my tongue. Her body reacted, letting her juices down and I drank from her like a dog at a spring.

Since she was knocked out and couldn't rail at me, I lapped and sucked at her pussy until my mouth grew tired and my dick was hard enough to cut steel. Her mind might be asleep but her body was awake. She responded so beautifully, moving against my mouth, taking my tongue deep within her.

But as I got up between her legs with my dick in hand ready to seal the deal, I realized it wasn't as much fun, her not being awake. I wanted to look into her eyes when I

take her the first time. Wanted her with me when I plant the first little one in her.

Still, I had the problem of a hard cock and a full sac to take care of, so I got to rubbing my cock up and down her slit while sucking on her titties. I can't wait to taste her milk, to fuck her while feeding on her.

I could see my sons and daughters in her arms, see the love and joy on her face as she accepted her lot in life. The picture was so clear I almost spent right then and there.

Her pussy was wet and my cock was leaking pre-cum all over her hairy snatch. I rubbed the fat head of my fuck meat up and down her slit until I reached her slit hole while chewing on her nipples.

I left my cock at the mouth of her cunt just enjoying the enormity of being so close. On one of my downward swipes my cock dipped into her pussy, which was now open and I pushed just a little. The sensations made my head swim as I fought not to fuck my sleeping angel.

She moaned in her sleep bringing my attention to her mouth. Licking her lips to get them moist, I stuck my tongue in her mouth to play with hers while pushing just the tip of my cock inside her warm wet pussy hole.

Her flesh grabbed me like a glove as I fucked just that little bit of myself in and out of her. On its own her body moved to meet mine making it damn near impossible for me not to slam my fully erect cock into her waiting cunt.

I grabbed her ass and pulled her tighter against me as my teeth mauled her tits and before you know it I was cumming inside her virgin pussy. Right up against her hymen.

My dick was still hard at the thought of having my Angel all to myself so I settled down to have some fun. She wouldn't be up for a while so it would give me time to explore her body without interruption. Get to know all her little nooks and crannies.

I was mostly fascinated with her tits. They were nice and firm yes, but they were also ample enough to feed my sons when the time

came. My cock leaked onto her pussy lips at the thought of my own mouth feeding at her milky tits one day soon.

I ran my hand over her flat tummy, imagining the day when it swelled with my seed. I left little marks on her body, from just beneath her nipple to her cute little belly button. I pulled out of her to explore her body before slipping back in, still careful not to pop her cherry.

All these things kept me in a state of arousal and I played with her body to my heart's content, doing anything and everything, except fucking her. I even lifted her legs as high as the rope would allow and fingered her tight little ass.

When I wasn't shoving my tongue in her pussy because I'd become addicted to the taste of her pussy juice, I was chewing on her tits and fingering her asshole. It was during one of those times when I was fingering her asshole while licking her pussy with my nuts full of spunk that I got the idea the take her ass while she was out.

Getting to my knees, I nosed around her little pink rose with my dick. Her ass was still wet from the fertility pill I'd put in her earlier and the pre-cum and spunk I'd leaked in her so it was easy enough to get the fat head of my cock inside her tight sphincter.

I planted my hands next to her head and slid my cock deep into her ass. "Damn that's some good ass." I tightened my gut and counted to ten so that I wouldn't cum too soon and once I had myself under control I got down to some serious ass fucking.

Chapter 8

T-Bone

***

When I'd cum about the fourth time I was plum worn out. After cleaning up after cumming in her ass, I'd rubbed my cock all over her exposed body, even letting it sit on her lips and coaxing her tongue to lick me in her sleep, I especially liked that.

Her tummy was covered in cum, so was her tits and hair and there was some drying on her thighs. I couldn't wait until she woke up so I could do it all over again.

The dawning light outside told me it was late, or early however you looked at it; time to get some rest. I laid beside her and pulled the covers up over us both, pulling her into my arms as best I could with her body still tied to the bed.

For the first time since daddy died and left me I felt at peace. I wasn't going to have to live out my days alone, and since no one knew

she was here, there would be no one to interfere with my happiness.

Now that she was here, I could breathe easy. Tomorrow, I'll get started on breeding her. That was for sure the quickest way to keep her with me. I knew enough about her life to know she didn't have much of a choice.

Once I get her to see that she could be happy here with me, that there was nothing out there in the world she's always complaining about, I'm sure she'd learn to accept her new life.

I thought of all the things that I'd ordered to help with that. I'd read her social media posts intently and knew her likes. I even knew what she had on her wish lists at a few online stores.

Hopefully, the fact that I'd got them all for her would go a long way to softening her up. That or she'd think I'm a sick stalker, in which case she'd still be stuck with me. Oh well.

***

Melanie

⁂

I jerked awake the next morning and went to roll over before I remembered my plight. It all came flooding back when I felt the hard arm beneath my cheek. My mouth tasted like horse manure and I couldn't remember anything beyond being tied down.

I flung myself back and would've fallen had I not been tied to the posts. I pulled on the ropes around my wrists to no avail. "Quit that Angel. Let me see your hands, you've hurt yourself."

My eyes flew to the face of the man who'd captured me. I expected to see a grotesque monster but instead my eyes connected with the bluest eyes I'd ever seen. Last night had been too dark and that day in class he was all covered but...

He was...he looked like someone but I couldn't place who. Without the shades and his hair unbound, his face was much softer.

Without the glasses hiding his eyes he didn't seem so scary.

I searched his face and my heart beat wildly for another reason. It would be just like me to get a crush on my own abductor. His gaze was making me feel all squishy inside. He had an intense stare, like he could see into me.

I squirmed under that heated look and shifted as much as my bonds would allow. It was then I realized that my body felt different. "Did you...what did you do to me?"

He turned his body completely towards me and I tried scooting away but found myself hauled back into his chest. "I did not violate you Melanie. I did touch you, but I restrained myself from taking your virginity while you were asleep."

"How do you know I'm a virgin?" He put his hand between my thighs and I felt his fingers slip inside me. He pressed against my hymen and my eyes widened. "I felt it, saw it."

My body reddened from my chest to my cheeks and I struggled to free myself again. "You looked inside me you sick bastard? Who the fuck looks inside someone's hoo-hah while they're asleep?" He really is crazy. He doesn't look it, and those eyes...

"Shh, you mustn't talk like that it'll teach the children bad manners." He tried to kiss me and I twisted my face away, which was a wasted effort since he grabbed my cheek and forced my mouth open with his tongue.

His hand covered my breast as he ravaged my mouth. I expected rough inept groping, but instead his hand cupped me gently while his thumb played with my nipple in the most sensual way. I held out, fighting the warring feelings inside, but then his hand travelled down-down, until it was back between my thighs and his thumb caressed my clit that had ever only known my hands, while his fingers drove inside of me again.

There was something about the way he touched me. Why wasn't he pawing at me, forcing himself on me like a rutting beast? I felt

every movement of his fingers and they weren't the fingers of a man bent on causing pain.

I was confused and aroused as my body moved on its own, following his lead. He touched me like he knew my body and I wondered just how much time he'd spent 'playing' with me while I slept.

"Cum for me Angel." The fingers inside of me sped up as the thumb on my clit moved in a circular motion that was maddening. Something sharp and intense rushed through me and my body bowed off the bed driving his fingers deeper as I came harder than I ever have in my life.

As soon as I came down shame and anger took over and I tried once more to pull away from him. "I don't want this, please let me go."

Chapter 9

T-Bone

***

I'd lain there for the better part of the morning waiting for my woman to wake up. My cock had been hard and hurting, but I didn't want a repeat of the night before. The next time I put my dick in her, I wanted her awake and burning for me.

She'd just cum for me, her body responding the way I'd dreamed, but my fingers weren't going to get me what I really wanted from her. I ignored her harsh words and she struggled some as I slid down the bed and placed myself between her spread legs, but a quick nip to her inner thigh soon had her holding still.

I spread her pretty pussy open with my fingers in search of her clit, which was still swollen. She pushed into my hand and bit into her lip to hold back her moans of pleasure.

"Where are my manners? Morning Angel." I swooped down with my mouth and sucked her clit into my mouth while easing three work-roughened fingers inside her pussy this time instead of two. She winced at the abrasion and I apologized as I pulled them out of her.

"Sorry sweetheart, where's my head." I pushed my fingers in her mouth. "Suck." She had no choice but to do as I said. When my fingers were nice and wet I pulled them from her mouth and slipped them back into her pussy.

"That's better." I went back to licking her clit and fingering her cunt until she was grinding her pussy against my face and fighting to keep her moans and screams of fulfillment behind her teeth.

I was sure having a fine time eating out the fresh virgin cunt beneath me. If I didn't know that her breeding time was close, I would've spent at least a week just licking her pussy, but I needed to get my dick inside her soon.

JORDAN SILVER

Reaching over to the table for the bag I'd brought home from the pharmacy, I retrieved another one of the bullet shaped tablets from its wrapper. "What are you doing?" She tried to escape my hands as I lifted her ass in the air.

"Shh. These are just to help your body along some." I slipped the fertility tablet into her ass and pushed it as deep inside her as possible. I did like the instructions said and gave it some time to dissolve while I played in her ass and ate her pussy.

I was proud of myself. Of the fact that my control had held this long. The scent of her pussy was thick in the air and the way she moved filled my head with visions of rutting inside her.

When the residue from the suppository started leaking from her ass I knew it had done what it was supposed to. Getting to my knees between her thighs with cock in hand I looked down at her frightened eyes.

She started screaming before I even touched her pussy with the fat head of my cock.

I knew that no amount of talking was going to make my task any easier, so I figured it was just like ma use to say when it came time to take a band aid off one of my cuts. Do it quick fast and be done.

I watched as my cock split her pussy lips open before they closed around the head, and sank in. "Heaven. I knew it would be good. Knew you were the one. My own Angel." I pulled back and worked my cock inside her, going deeper each time, weakening her maidenhead for the final stroke.

I covered her mouth with mine before slamming into her hard, tearing through her innocence, making her mine, and caught her screams in my mouth.

I held still to give her time to adjust to having me inside her. "Shh, it's okay, you're okay now sweet Angel." I kissed her cheek softly and waited for her to calm down.

***

JORDAN SILVER

Melanie

***

It felt like he was shoving a hot poker inside me. My skin burned and ached from being stretched and I couldn't believe that it was just his cock in there. He held still as if giving me time to adjust to his invasion, but there was no way.

Realistically I knew it was just his cock, and that I couldn't die from losing my virginity but at that moment you couldn't convince me of that. I've never been this full, or felt so much pain.

I opened my mouth to scream again when he started to move, and all of a sudden the burning pressure was gone. I opened my eyes and looked down between my thighs in time to see him lifting me to his mouth.

I was struck dumb for the first few seconds and then the most incredible feeling sent shockwaves through my body and

centered right between my thighs where he was tasting me with his tongue.

I couldn't help it, my body moved in the most sensuous way as I tried to get more of his tongue in me. My hips moved wildly and I moaned wantonly, almost begging him for more as his tongue did the most amazing things inside me. I almost said the words, 'fuck me', they were on the tip of my tongue; and then the light went off.

What? What's going on? I fought my body's traitorous need, told myself that if my hands weren't tied I would be fighting him instead of laying here like this letting him use me like this.

I tried to think of anything to take my mind away, tried reminding myself that I wasn't here by choice and he was a criminal who'd stolen me and brought me here to violate me. But none of it worked.

No matter what I did, I couldn't stop my hips from lifting off the bed and pressing my pussy harder against his mouth. I tried holding

back the screams of ecstasy but it was no use, my body was already shaking in orgasmic bliss.

No sooner had one bolt of lightning hit than another one followed and right in the middle of it, he took away the sweet-sweet pleasure of his tongue and slid his big fat cock back into me.

This time there was hardly any pain. I waited with breath held for the sting of discomfort but instead felt...pleasure? Just as I was getting ready to yell at him to get off of me, he lowered his head and took my nipple into his mouth. "Oh...oh...uhhhhhhhhh."

My body went up in flames and my face turned red at the sounds I made. My body wouldn't stop, couldn't stop. And no matter how hard he pounded into me, or how deep he went, I wanted more. This wasn't right, I shouldn't...

"Please...no...stop." What's happening to me? And why was he being so tender? So loving? When what I'd been expecting from the rough looking character was anything but.

"Fuck Angel that's the sweetest damn pussy I ever had wrapped around my cock. You want me to stop, huh? Then why is your cunt so wet?" He did something with his hair, flung his head back to get it out of his face and that's when I knew who he reminded me of.

Warm liquid pooled between my thighs and ran down the thick hard pole that moved inside me. He looked like that biker guy from the TV show. A handsome guy like him shouldn't need to grab women off the street.

My mind was dragged back to the here and now when he shifted his body at an angle almost crosswise over my chest and with his face buried in my neck and my flesh caught between his teeth, hit something inside me that made stars explode in my head.

"Ahhhhhhhhh." The scream tore out of me and echoed around the room. His grunts and groans made me feel exhilarated, sexy; slutty. I wanted to fuck him. My body moved along with my thoughts and before I knew it I was moving just as wildly as he was.

He liked that. He held my hips and fucked into me like he couldn't get enough. "Fuck Angel here it comes, our first baby. Take my seed." His words were like a bucket of ice cold water in my face. I woke from my trance and realized what I'd said, what I'd done.

I pulled against the restraints and willed my body to stop its traitorous behavior. When he lowered his head to kiss me I turned my face away in a show of defiance. Still my body moved on its own and his chuckle smacked of victory.

"I hate you get off me." He stopped moving and I thought I'd got through to him. I didn't stop to think what he'd do to me for defying him, yelling at him.

I held my breath to see what he would do next and felt tears prick my lashes. My hands were so well tied I had no hope of escaping whatever he had planned.

Chapter 10

T-Bone

***

I stopped all movement and looked into her eyes. Her words cut me deep. No one had ever said they hated me before and though I knew it would take some time for her to come around, I never considered that she might actually hate me.

The only thing that gave me hope in that moment was the way her body responded to me. I knew enough to know that a woman or a man's body for that matter might react without their say-so, but I knew that what she'd just felt, the way she just lit up beneath me was more than that.

I wasn't troubled. I knew just how to make her body betray her and out a stop to her lip. Pulling out of her snug gash, I lowered my mouth to her and tongued her pussy deep.

I didn't just eat her pussy, this time I closed my eyes and made love to her as was

fitting the woman that would be the mother of my children, the wife of my heart.

I licked inside her slowly while massaging her thighs. She tried holding out, lashing out at me with that sharp tongue of hers, but I could already feel the give in her body.

She relaxed beneath my hands and mouth, I don't even think she noticed. Pulling my tongue out of her, I teased her clit with just the tip until she whimpered. I smiled at the sound and went back to eating her sweet pussy, fucking her with my tongue, with nice slow deep strokes.

I curled my tongue up as if searching for something. I wanted all her sweet juice on my tongue. I could very well live off of it for the rest of my days it was that good.

She'd stopped tugging against the ropes around her wrists and ankles, and I doubted that she even realized that she was making those sexy little noises or that she was now

pushing her bush into my mouth. Begging me without words to eat her out.

I would've been happy to leave my tongue buried in the sweet pussy beneath me, but my cock had other ideas. My poor bone was about to break in half if I didn't slide it back into her wet honeypot.

I brought her to the edge again and just as she was in the middle of another intense orgasm, slid up her body, covered her mouth with mine, and slid my cock home, going deep until I bottomed out.

I needed to get into her womb, where my seed would stand a better chance. That, along with the fertility drugs I planned to insert in her ass everyday until I bred her were my guarantee that this will work fast.

She didn't have any medical issues that would prohibit her from carrying my child, there was nothing standing in the way. And I was sure my seed was strong enough to do the job.

JORDAN SILVER

"We're going to make such beautiful babies Angel." I pulled her head back and kissed her as I thrust my cock into her harder and harder, preparing her tight little pussy for what I knew was coming.

***

Melanie

***

His words scared and aroused me at the same time. Each time I tried to hold onto a thought, to find the one thing that would awaken me from this madness that had taken over my body, he'd say or do something to drag me back into the lust filled haze that clouded my mind.

I had no recourse against the onslaught. I've listened to my girlfriends talk over the years and not once had I ever heard of anything like this.

Instead of the selfish, oafish hurried actions of the boys they'd complained about, this mountain man took his time. He used his

tongue inside my sex like he really thought there was something in there for him to feast on, and now he was moving inside me like I was his greatest pleasure.

'This may hurt a little Angel. I have to get into your womb now. Forgive me." What was he talking about? I started to freak out wondering if he meant to slice me open. But then he grabbed my hips between his large callused hands, pulled almost all the way out of me before slamming back in...hard.

My mouth opened but no sound came. The pain was like nothing I'd ever known, not even when he'd breached me the first time. But right on its heels was a pleasure so intense I couldn't describe it.

He eased out of that place and I felt sweet relief only to be taken up in the maelstrom again when he surged back in.

He lifted my ass in his hands and pushed himself in and out of me being careful not to hurt me. "That's it Angel don't that feel good?" He didn't wait for an answer, but his

finger came down to pleasure my clit. I bit into my lip to hold the screams of pleasure inside.

I didn't know what to do. This was wrong, wasn't it? Shouldn't I hate this, hate him? But why was he able to make my body feel this way? How could I enjoy what he was doing to me? I felt new tears prick my eyes even as my body, still under his complete control, opened to accept him.

"Don't cry love, it's going to be okay." He licked the tears from my eyes as he moved inside me. "I'm going to remove your bonds now, you'll be more comfortable." He stopped long enough to remove the ropes from my arms and legs

"Better?" He kissed me like we were lovers, and when I tried pulling away he nipped my lip until I stopped fighting him. "Don't fight me Melanie, I don't want to tie you up again."

How could his words strike such fear when his body offered only pleasure? If he was rough with me, maybe then I could get my body to act the way it should.

With that thought in mind, I started to fight him. Ignoring the feelings between my thighs, the pleasure he gave me, I scraped my nails down his back and bucked my hips in an effort to throw him off. He was lodged so deep inside me I was wasting my time. I screamed abuse at him, called him every vile name I could think of

He stopped with a stunned look on his face. I braced myself and waited for the blow but instead he grabbed both my hands in his and held them above my head as he marked my neck with his teeth. I felt it in my womb, the sweet pull, and in one last ditch effort to save myself, tried using my freed legs to hurt him.

He pulled out of me so quickly I didn't know what he was doing until I found myself turned roughly onto my stomach. "I'm going to fuck you until you learn to mind me." With that he slammed his cock into me.

The scream got trapped in my lungs this time and his hand around my throat didn't help. "I hate you, why are you doing this to

me?" My hands were free and so I reached back and tried to gouge his eyes out.

I was expecting him to retaliate harshly but instead his touch became gentler, his whispers more those of a lover than the kidnapping bastard he was. "If you hurt yourself I'll be forced to tie you down to the bed again. Is that what you want, huh?"

He kept fucking into me as he spoke and then his hand came around and teased my clit. "Open your legs for me Angel." When I didn't move fast enough he bit my ear. "Don't make me have to tell you again. I don't like repeating myself."

When he made a jabbing motion with his cock that was meant to hurt I opened my legs which pushed my ass back hard into him. That only gave him a better angle to fuck deeper into my womb.

Those sweet feelings started in the pit of my stomach again and I just let go, what was the use? I'll fight later, when my body wasn't racked with pleasure. I moved into his thrusts.

Once I decided to give in to this my body just took over and went where it wanted to.

"That's my good girl." He kept whispering things in my ear, things that made my blood hot and my pussy wet. His hand between my thighs, pressing on my clit, his teeth in my neck, leaving his mark, made me lock down around him until I came.

He sped up his thrusts and licked the sting in my neck and the sound that came from me was one I'd never heard before. It was low, guttural; primal. When he went back into that place deep inside again the whole world went black.

Chapter 11

T-Bone

***

I slid out of her body when she went limp and turned her onto her back. She was breathing just fine so I figured she'd just had a fainting spell. I took the time while she was out to head to the bathroom for a washcloth to clean her up.

Once in there, I saw her blood on my cock and cleaned myself up first. I heard a noise coming from the bedroom and dashed back in there just in time to see her bare ass booking it out the door. "Well shit!" I forgot to lock the damn door.

I saw her shredded clothes on the chair where I'd left them the night before and took my tine going after her. There was nowhere for her to run. I got outside and saw her in the middle of the yard turning round and round looking for an escape.

I leaned against the open door and watched her. "Come on back in here before you catch your death of cold Angel." I had a hankering for some canned peaches, and it was time I fed her.

She took one look at me and took off running. "Well shit!" I looked down at my dick that was swinging in the wind and then back at where she was headed hell bent for leather.

I didn't have time to grab my jeans off the bedroom floor. Her naked ass was headed right for the poison ivy. I hopped on my ATV and yelped at the cold seat as it hit my ass and balls, and went after her. She looked back and ran faster but her little legs were no match for my ride.

I pulled around in front of her and revved the engine, going up on the two front wheels. She jumped a foot in the air before trying to walk around me. I put the wheels back on the ground, leaned over and reached out to snatch her off her feet. "No let me go put me down."

"Stop it." I smacked her ass hard and threw her across my lap with her kicking and screaming. She sure did have some lungs on her for such a little thing. She squirmed around on my lap and my dick went on full alert.

I should really get her back inside out the cold but...I slipped my fingers inside her and she stopped cold, but not for long. I strummed her pussy nice and slow until her juices filled my hand. I turned her over and sat her on my cock, pulling her down until her ass hit my thighs.

She opened her mouth to rail at me again but I didn't give her a chance. Leaning her backward onto the handlebars I took one of her nipples into my mouth and sucked hard as I surged up into her.

I wrapped my arms tightly around her as I fucked and soon forgot the cold. Her body moved on its own and pretty soon she was riding my cock like my own little cowgirl.

It gave me an idea but that was for another time. It would have to be soon though, I wouldn't risk fucking her on the back of my ornery horse when she's with child.

"We have to hurry Angel it's cold out here. Cum." I tickled her puckered rosebud and she went wild, working my dick until he was spitting inside her. She shook from the cold and I used one hand to hold her and the other to ride us back to the house with my dick snug inside her.

We walked inside like that with my cock still buried deep in her. The movement kept my dick hard as I made my way back to the unmade bed. Once I had her under me I pulled her legs up over my shoulders and fucked into her for the next hour bringing her off over and over again.

I made sure she was good and tired this time but I still didn't leave her alone. Instead, I took her into the bathroom and turned on the shower for both of us.

Her body was a mess. She had love bites on her chest, her back; her ass. Her hair was wild and untamed from my hands, and she was never more beautiful.

She didn't help at all while I washed her before taking care of myself. Once out of the shower I opened the drawer I'd cleared just for her and showed her what I had there.

She looked at all the creams and gook that women seem not able to live without. Her eyes flew to mine in shocked surprise. "What is this?"

"Isn't that what you wanted?" I put some toothpaste on both our brushes and turned on the water in my sink. "But how did you know?" "It was on your wish list love."

I started brushing while she just stood there. "You need to hurry up Angel it's time for your breakfast." I finished up and threw on my robe. "Your robe is right there Angel." I kissed her temple before walking out of the room.

In the kitchen, I started the flapjacks batter while keeping my ears tuned to her every move down the hall. I heard the water running which meant she was brushing her teeth but right on the back of that I heard the dog barking wildly.

I dropped the mixing spoon and ran down the hall to the bathroom. The window was open. "How the hell did she fit through there?" I hadn't secured it because I stupidly didn't think she could.

I tightened my robe and walked around to the front door. Rex wouldn't bite her unless I told him to, but she wouldn't know that, and she'd be scared.

She was backed up to the house holding the robe closed, her bare feet on the cold ground. "Don't move Angel. Rex down." I'll introduce the two of them later once she was settled in.

I didn't say anything to her as I picked her up gently in my arms and hurried back inside. I put her down and dragged her into the

kitchen. "Sit. If you get up from that chair I'm gonna tie you to my bed again." I was thinking it's a good thing that she'd seen first hand that she couldn't escape, that there was no one around to help her.

"You don't wanna go running in them woods back there. I have bear traps set up all over the place but every once in a while one gets by them and make his way all the way up to the front door." She went white as a sheet.

"Nothing to be afraid of, I'll protect you." I got the pot and put on some milk to heat up for her before getting the ground coffee out. She was spitting mad as her pretty eyes followed me around the room.

"I want to go home."
"No. This is your home now. I got you some magazines and stuff so you can buy whatever you need to make the place nice for you and the kids. Come spring, I'm thinking I might add on another room. There's only three bedrooms now and with six kids that's not gonna be enough room. Especially if they're not all boys."

Her mouth dropped clear to her chest but I pretended not to notice. "Are you insane?" I gave that some thought since she deserved an honest answer. "No I don't think so." I took the milk off the stove before it boiled over and poured her a mug.

"I'm not drinking anything you made." "Nothing in there but milk. I won't be giving you anymore of those pills, scared me half to death the way you just keeled over like that. Besides, they can't be any good for a woman with child."

I heated the griddle and made us both a nice breakfast of flapjacks and eggs. She'd let her milk cool so I reheated it a bit and pulled her up from her seat before sitting there myself.

"Open." I held the mug to her lips and ran my hand up between her thighs under the robe. She obeyed me until the cup was empty. "Now eat." She picked up her fork and started eating, small little nibbles meant to annoy me I guess.

JORDAN SILVER

Once breakfast was over, I took her back to the bedroom and laid her across the bed. "Time for another suppository Angel." I was already late feeding the animals and since I promised not to tie her up again unless she misbehaved I guess I had to take her with me.

I slipped the pill in her ass thinking that would be the end of it, but her robe fell open and with her legs in the air, her bush pepping through her thighs at me, it wasn't long before my dick was hard for her again.

I kept her legs up and licked her pussy. "I have to shave you Angel. I love your curly bush but it's getting in my teeth. Keep your legs up like that for me Angel." I let go of her legs and opened her pussy with my fingers.

She was pink and soft and beautiful. I let my tongue play inside her until my cock couldn't take it anymore. I stood to my feet and led my cock into her. Her short legs barely reached the top of my shoulders as I spread her legs open with my hips and fucked.

She moved wildly, enjoying the fucking I was giving her as her tits bounced on her chest with every stroke. "You're here for my pleasure, I'm going to make a baby in you." Her eyes flew to mine and I could see the war inside her.

I knew now that she couldn't keep her body's reaction from me, that she couldn't control the way she responded to having my cock or my tongue in her.

"It's best if you give in, if you accept. If you continue to fight I will punish you Angel, but if you give in I will give you everything that I am. I took your virginity, that means you belong to me now and no one else will ever have you not ever.

Now touch yourself."

I knew she was going to defy me before she did it, but the hand around her throat had her hand moving down between her legs and onto her clit.

"That's a good girl." I knew I would never hurt her, but she didn't know that, and I

was willing to do whatever it took to get her to accept her fate.

Her fingers on her clit were doing their job because it wasn't long before her pussy tightened around me and I felt her juices start to flow. "You love my cock don't you Angel?" I didn't expect an answer, I'll let her body do the talking for her.

Leaning over, I took her nipple into my mouth, driving my cock deeper. I sucked hard on her nipple before letting it pop out of my mouth. I knew that words sometimes more than actions would get her to see and accept faster.

"I can't wait 'til my sons and daughters get to feed on you like this." I swallowed her tit again and fucked her pussy nice and deep as she meditated on those words.

I painted a picture in her head with whispered words of all the things I was going to do to her. Her pussy made me feel ten feet tall. I'd expected to have a warm body next to mine in the years to come. Had imagined the

children we will have together, but I couldn't have imagined what it would feel like to be inside of her, this particular beauty.

I hadn't wanted just any woman, I know that now. No one else would've done. I felt something more than just a warm body that could carry my seed. As I looked down at her, felt her around my cock, I saw the future. My heart opened and let her in then and there.

The feelings, the emotion was so raw I almost killed the poor girl. My thrusts became harder, faster, more forceful as I drove my cock even deeper into her, butting against her cervix until it opened and let me in to the mouth of her womb.

She grunted with each thrust of my hips and her ass didn't stay still. The bed rocked with each stroke of my cock into her depths and her pussy clung each time I squeezed around her neck.

"That's it doesn't that feel good?" She may not like the circumstances but my little girl

sure did love cock no matter how she spat harsh words at me or accused me with her eyes.

I grinned down at her before leaning over to take her lips. She got sassy and tried keeping her tongue from me but a nip to her lip soon made her yelp and open up.

"Don't ever keep yourself from me." Her hot little pussy juiced at my rough treatment of her and gave me ideas. Oh yes, it was going to be fun breaking her to my will, making her a slave to my loving. "Do you want my seed in your belly little Melanie? Do you want me to put my baby in you now?"

I knew she wouldn't answer, but used the words to enflame her. A woman, no matter who she is, is programmed to want her man to breed her, as often as possible too.

The truth of that was evident when she almost lifted me off of her as her body arched hard and her hips fucked up at me harder, faster, wilder as she came. She screamed so loud Rex started up a howling outside.

I slammed her body back down onto the mattress with mine as my cock went off like a pistol, hosing down her insides with my seed.

"Yes Angel, that's it, that's a good girl." She made the cutest little rutting noises as her skin grew fever hot and her eyes glazed over with lust.

"What did you do to me? There was something in the milk." She'd like to think so, anything but accepting that her body liked what I did to it.

"No Angel, that was all you, you love fucking. I'm thinking it's lucky I came along when I did or who knows what low life loser you'd have ended up with."

She had a few choice words for me which I ignored with a grin. "Now listen, I have to go feed the animals. I was going to take you with me, but I'm thinking it might be too cold out there and that jacket you were wearing isn't going to keep you warm and mine are way too big for you to be any good. I'll see about

ordering you one when I get back." I looked at her as I made up my mind.

"Come with me." I didn't wait to see if she would obey, just turned for the door. "Don't make me have to come get you Angel." I smiled at the sound of her little feet hitting the floor.

"Where are you taking me now?" I took her to the back room where I'd stored most of the stuff I'd bought to make the place suitable for female company. I opened the door and moved out of the way for her to go on in.

"You can spend your time fixing up the place to suit. If there's anything you need just let me know and I'll see to it." She looked around the room and then back at me.

"Did you steal this stuff?" She would like that, another reason for her to resist me. I didn't tell her that I was rich, I didn't want her making up her mind on account of that.

When she decided that she wanted to stay I wanted it to be because of me. I'll settle

for her falling in love with my cock more so than if it was my money that turned the tide.

"No. Now do you promise to be a good girl and stay put while I go tend the livestock? Rex will be right outside the door and if I'm not here to call him off he just might eat you before I get back in time to stop him."

That put fear in her and I saw the wheels turning. "You shouldn't have to sic your dog on a woman to keep her, that's pathetic."
"You could be right about that. But what's more pathetic, a man who sees what he wants and goes after it, or one who fiddles around like a newborn babe not sure of himself or what he wants?"

"What's the divorce rate out there again? Your mama was married three times and had a whole lot of boyfriends. You'll only ever know one man in your whole life. One that will never mistreat you or treat our children the way you were treated." I smirked at the look of disbelief on her face as I turned to walk away.

"How did you...?"

"I know everything about you. Think about that whenever you think about escaping. There's nowhere you can go that I won't find you." I walked out of the room and headed out the door to see about the farm.

Chapter 12

Melanie

***

For the next three days we had a routine. At least he had one. I was just the little puppet on his string. Every night after he took my body he made me sleep next to him, wrapped tightly in his arms with one of his legs thrown over mine. He might as well had tied me up again.

In the mornings, I woke to him already inside me or with his head between my thighs. Then he'd put one of those things in my ass twice a day. When we weren't eating, sleeping or feeding the animals he was inside me.

I was still trying to figure him out. He never raised his voice, never hit me, and even when I got frustrated and hauled off and slugged him a time or two all he did was kiss me and take me to bed, and once on the kitchen table.

He talked about the farm, the future; our kids. Everything and anything except the one thing I wanted to know. Whenever I brought up the subject of him letting me go he just ignored me, or changed the subject.

And sometimes at night, he'd sing to me. He had an old guitar that he said belonged to his daddy and he'd taught himself how to play. His favorite song was Moon River from some movie I'd never heard of.

I wouldn't tell him, but he had a beautiful voice. It put me at peace. He could go on and on for hours about the land and all the things he had planned for us and our as yet unborn children. Sometimes I could even see it plain as day.

Last night for the first time I was eager to get to bed. I wanted him and didn't know what to do about that turn of events. It felt like maybe I should be trying harder to get away, not giving in to my plight.

I laid in bed early the next morning looking at the sunrise through the window

while he laid behind me with his arms holding me tight. "Are you awake Angel?" He kissed my ear and squeezed me. "Isn't this much better? Can you hear the birds singing? Do you see the sun climbing over the top of the tree line?"

Every morning he did this. It was as if he was trying to sell me on the idea of living here. I was afraid I was losing my will to fight, but every time I felt that way I just dug my heels in and fought all the harder.

I moved to get out of bed but his hands pulled me back. My body reacted, already preparing itself for his. I was becoming conditioned and he knew it the bastard.

"Lift your leg Angel." I don't know why he asked since he did it himself before sliding into me from behind. I bit my lip so the sigh of pleasure wouldn't escape but I should've known he wouldn't let that slide.

He turned my head to him and licked across my lips while moving deeper into me and my mouth opened to accept him. His big

rough hand squeezed my breast as he moved slowly back and forth.

Mornings were the worst. It's then he takes his time as if the three or four times he'd had me throughout the night had taken the edge off and he could take his time and make me crazy.

It was times like these that I felt like what we were doing was so much more than having sex. I felt tears prick my eyes as those sweet feelings started in the pit of my tummy. I still didn't know how he was able to get me to react to his touch when I was against everything he stood for.

Yesterday, I'd found myself wanting him, missing his touch while he was outside with the animals while I stayed back rearranging the furniture and putting up curtains.

I knew what was happening to me, knew that I was falling for him. That the tenderness he showed me was breaking down all my walls.

"Stop thinking so hard Melanie Angel, just feel."

His hand moved down between my legs and found my clit. "Oh…" I pushed back hard and sucked on his tongue even harder as my hips sped up. My heart felt like it would burst in my chest and I was crying loud broken sobs when he pushed me onto my stomach and drove into me.

It was so good, I can't deny that what he does to my body surpasses all expectations. I was tired of holding back, tired of fighting against myself. Just this once I told myself. Just this once I will let myself enjoy.

It's as if as soon as I made up my mind my body took over. "That's my good girl." I pushed back against him sliding myself on and off his cock as he squeezed my nipple with one hand and tormented my clit with the fingers of the other.

***

T-Bone

***

I fucked into my pussy hard from behind, pulling her slender hips back into my groin as I pummeled her sweet cunt. I felt the change in her and smiled. This is what I was waiting for, once I got her to give into me only once I knew I had her for a lifetime.

"Should I breed you like this? Is this the best way to create our child do you think?" Her pussy locked down on my cock and her back arched until her chest met the mattress trapping my hand under her.

"Please-please-please." She cried and pleaded. "Tell me what you want Angel say it."

"Fuck me, fuck me fuck me." I growled and lifted her off her knees sinking my dick deeper inside her over and over, until I howled out my orgasm. I rode it out in her until my seed was all gone and her harsh breathing was coming back to normal.

She tried hiding from me after that but I didn't let her. I didn't bring up her capitulation

as I took her from the bed to clean her up in the shower. Now that I'd made that little leeway I didn't fool myself into thinking that she was through fighting me.

In fact, I expected her to fight me even harder now that her body had gone over to the enemy. She'd have to fight, to convince herself that she hadn't given into who she saw as her captor.

I kept my eyes on her once we were out of the shower. "It's your turn to make breakfast today." I've only been letting her wear one of my old shirts in the house for added warmth since the temperature had dropped outside. It wasn't time for her to wear anything more, not until after I'd bred her at least.

She didn't say a word to me as she marched into the kitchen and started banging the pots around. I hid my grin as I took my place at the table. I wonder if she realized that it was barely four thirty in the morning.

We had our breakfast and then I bundled her up to take her with me. I had to

cover a heifer with the bull this morning and I didn't know how long I would be. Seeing as how she had something new on her mind this morning after begging me to fuck her I thought it best to remove all temptation.

I hurried us to the barn and put her a safe distance out of the way. "You stay over here in case he gets ornery." Samson was one of the old stud's offspring and truth be known was twice the stud his daddy had been which was saying a lot.

I tied the heifer off, moving slow because I knew she was watching my every move from the corner I'd sat her in. Samson walked up to the heifer who was in heat and sniffed her to get her scent.

He licked her flank and laid his head on her rump before jumping up behind her. His rod poked out and went into her as his front legs held her in place.

I heard her breathing change behind me and watched long enough for Samson to get inside the heifer before turning back to her.

As the bull started his wild thrusting into the heifer I moved around behind Angel and stripped the coat from her shoulders. I pushed her down to the hay facing the animals and got behind her and once her jeans were out of the way, mounted her.

She was wet and hot as her gaze remained transfixed on the animals. Samson rutted the heifer viciously and I timed my thrusts in her pussy to keep pace with him. Her pussy gushed and she screamed along with the heifer as I fucked her hard and deep.

"Do you see how beautiful mating is Angel? This is how we will make our babies. I know you're in heat it's the perfect time to breed you." She pushed back hard at my words as her hands stretched in front of her and she dug her knees into the straw.

Her mind was gone now, lost in the world of animal lust. "That's it, fuck my cock; take all you need." I pulled back and slammed into her hard going into her womb where it was getting easier for her to take me.

She fisted the straw in her hands and fucked herself harder on my cock as her head went back and her mouth hung open in primal lust and pleasure. I came harder than ever before, the flesh of her neck caught between my teeth as I fucked the last of my seed inside her.

"We'll stay like this a little longer." I wrapped my arms around her middle holding her back to my chest as our breathing evened out. Only then did I slip out of her tight cunt.

"Now you can help me feed the animals." She didn't say a word, just walked to the food barrel and started filling the troughs while I got the hose and filled the others with water.

We worked together in silence and I pretended not to notice her secret stares. When I did look at her she'd look away shyly with her face red, but I noticed her nipples were still hard.

When we got back to the house it was she who attacked me. "Calm down Angel I'll take you just let me get out of my boots." She

was moaning low in her throat and her movement were disjointed and rash.

I barely got my boots and jeans off intending to take her to the bed, but she pushed me back against the wall and covered my mouth with hers.

I knew of course what had brought this on, it's why I'd taken her out there in the first place. She rubbed her naked tits into my chest and I knew they must be hurting for want of attention. I took over and pushed her back a little so I could get to them.

She sighed when I sucked the first one deep into my mouth, pressing it against the roof of my mouth with my tongue. Her pussy rubbed against my cock and I could feel her pussy juice leak all over me. "Let me take you to the bed little darling."

She grunted and before I knew it she was on her knees in front of me looking back over her shoulder with a look of such need on her face that I felt my heart squeeze.

I dropped to my knees behind her and licked her pussy until she reached back and grabbed my hair. "Okay-okay." I got up behind her and pushed my cock into her going balls deep with one thrust.

"Is this what you want?" She was wild and untamed and I knew she was seeing the bull fuck the heifer. Upstaged by a damn cow.

When I cupped her tits this time she shivered as if they were too tender. Her insides were softer than before, she was in the middle of her breeding cycle.

The thought that I could even now be planting my seed in her, a seed that would grow was too much and I came almost as fast as the bull. I know I damn sure came just as hard.

She didn't seem able to move so I picked her up and took her to bed. "Your titties hurt Angel?" I knew a lot more about a woman's body than half the married men out there. I'd made it a point to read up on that stuff.

I knew that she would be tender this time of the month. I laid her on her back and slid my cock back into her and spent the next half hour sucking her nipples until she cried.

"Now I'm going to fuck you." I kept sucking her tits one after the other while pummeling her sweet hot cunt with my iron hard cock.

"Cum for me like a good girl." She bit me and held me closer wrapping her legs and arms around me to keep me locked into her embrace. I kept fucking into her long after I'd cum and she laid beneath me cooing.

"That was beautiful Angel thank you." I kissed her lips softly intending only a quick passing of my lips over hers. But she opened her mouth so softly, so sweetly and ran her tongue across my lips before slipping it into my mouth.

I almost crushed her in my eagerness as the kiss went on forever. I left my cock inside her as we kissed each other hungrily and her hands roamed over my back and chest.

"I need you again baby." I kept my lips locked with hers as I reached beneath her to grab her ass lifting her into my thrusts.

I felt like I was deeper in her than I'd ever been. My arms were wrapped around her so tight is was as if we were one and the hungry little sounds she made drove me mad. "I want you to cum with me."

I eased the tip of my finger past her tight sphincter and her pussy clamped and throbbed until we both exploded. Me with a loud roar and she with a guttural growl as her arms and legs tightened around me.

I slid out of her and dropped to my side pulling her along with me. When we were both able to move again I took her into the bathroom and sat her on the edge of the tub.

I got daddy's old shaving kit ready and wet a washcloth with warm water while she watched. "Open." I pushed her legs apart and wet the hair on her pussy with the cloth, doing it twice more before I was satisfied.

I lathered some cream together and covered her bush before taking my time and scraping it off with the razor. "Don't move Angel, I may cut you." "It tickles."

"I know baby, not much more now." I cleaned all the hair from her until her pussy was bald. When I'd cleaned her all up, I couldn't resist sticking my tongue in her and eating her newly shaved pussy until she came on my tongue.

"There, we'll keep you nice and shaved from now on otherwise you'll itch when it starts to grow back." She was limp from all the day's exertions so I held her in the shower and washed us both off before pulling a pair of socks on over her feet and another one over mine.

We moved around the house like that for the rest of the day, even when I made her help me cook dinner that evening.

Every so often, I'd stop what I was doing and take her in my arms for a kiss, or rub my

fingers over her pussy before finger fucking her then having her lick her juices from my fingers.

I didn't say anything to her about the things I did to her or planned to do to her. Instead, I kept the conversation light and spoke of more mundane things.

We had a great discussion about the condition of the world and of course I used every opportunity to show her how much better her situation was here with me than out there.

That evening we watched the news together. I'd been keeping up with the news for a while, looking for any news about her disappearance. She didn't know but I did, that she had already been written off as a runaway. No one was looking for her.

That wasn't my reason for wanting her to watch the news though, her story was old news already. I wanted her to see what I see when I look at it. The degradation and depravity that exists in the world she moved in before she came to the peace and serenity of the farm.

"I like what you did with the old parlor. I don't think anyone has ever made it that pretty before." She was sitting on my lap with my hand fondling her tit as we looked at the tube.

"Thank you." I squeezed her nipple in answer and carried on watching.

For the next two weeks, I took her outside more and more. Once she rode my horse in front of me and I finally got to fuck her on his back.

And a few evenings, I had her sit behind me on the ATV. She took to both so well I promised to buy her-her own horse and ATV. She lit up at the offer and kissed my cheek.

"T-Bone, I'm ready for bed it's getting cold." I put down the book I was reading while she laid reading her own with her head on my lap.

"Okay, little darling let me make sure everything is locked up." She walked off into the bedroom while I secured the house before

joining her. She was in bed with the covers over her and the pillows at her back.

We'd got to using candles at night instead of electricity because it made everything seem so cozy and she'd lit the ones on her night table and mine. "Should we light the fire tonight you think, or is it still too warm?"

"Oh that would be nice." I already had the wood ready and all it took was adding some kindling and striking a match. I made sure it was fine before going around the bed to my side and climbing in under the covers.

I moved close to her back and wrapped my arm around her. Her hand reached for mine and pulled it higher over her breast. I caressed her as we talked about the coming winter and all the fun things there was to do around here this time of year.

She was excited for me to teach her how to can vegetables and make jam the way my mama had taught me. By the time she pushed back and slightly raised her leg I was already

hard as a pike and all it took was for me to angle my hips and slip my cock up inside her while we carried on our conversation.

Chapter 13

Melanie

***

I'm not sure when it happened, but I couldn't have been here that long when he started making sense. Every morning I woke up and went outside and the air was fresh and crisp. All around me was peace and quiet and the most beautiful land I'd ever seen.

T-Bone spent almost every second with me, teaching me things. I even learned how to milk the cows and find the eggs the hens laid for the day.

I was learning so much here, like how to make candles and soap, who knew that stuff could me so much fun? T-Bone had taught Rex how to accept me and now he just follows me around when I go outside instead of growling and carrying on, he was just a big old softie.

T-Bone taught me how to make the soda bread his mama used to make and we had fun with that and a whole lot of other things his

mama had taught him when he was just a little boy. My mom never taught me shit but how to be mean and to hate men.

The first morning I woke up and found jeans and the softest cashmere sweater thrown over the old rocker in the bedroom with new riding boots and a kickass shearling jacket I almost had a heart attack.

I ran into the kitchen where he was getting the coffee ready, sure I made a sight but I didn't care. "I'm not going back, you can't make me." I was already in tears and my little fists were clenched so tight I thought they would break.

"What is it Angel, did you have a bad dream?" He turned and came to me, taking me in his arms but I was mad as hell. I pounded his chest and yelled at him until he grabbed both my hands and held them in one of his.

"Stop that before you hurt yourself. Now tell me darling, what's wrong?"
"Why are you making me leave?" I hiccupped and bawled like an infant.

"What are you talking about? You're not going anywhere." I took his hand and dragged him down the hall to our bedroom and pointed to the clothes.

"Then what's that?"
"Well, it's a bit chilly in the house and you like the fire more than the gas heat and I don't want you catching your death of cold so I figured you should have something on other than socks. See, I'm wearing my sweats too."

I finally calmed down when I saw the truth of his words. He didn't laugh or make fun of the fact that I was crying to stay when only a few weeks ago I'd been begging to leave. He just took my hand and led me back to the kitchen.

"Sit, breakfast will be ready soon. I think Samson that old reprobate bred five heifers. Only two didn't catch but that's okay, he'll get them next time."

"That's great. T how many babies does a cow have?"

"Well now that depends. Most only have one calf at a time, but every once in a while you might find one who'd have two or maybe three."

"Oh okay. And how long is a cow pregnant for?"

"About the same amount of time as a woman give or take, forty weeks or so. I was just thinking if you caught our day in the barn then our baby should be coming just about the same time as that last one we saw bred."

My face went up in flames. He says stuff like that so casually, like it was the most natural thing in the world. "I don't think I'm pregnant." And why did that make me feel sad instead of overjoyed? I hadn't given my old life a second thought in days, weeks even and for some reason the thought of going back scared me.

"I was going to take care of that after breakfast." He dropped a box in front of me on the table and I saw that it was a pregnancy test. My heart felt sick and I realized it was the thought of disappointing him that was making me feel this way.

"What if I'm not?" My voice was low and sad. "Well then we'll just have to try until you are." I smiled and drank the warm milk he put in front of me.

***

T-Bone Nine Months Later

"I'm not going."
"Yes, you are and that's final Melanie."
"We'll see about that. I'm not going to no hospital for no doctor to paw at me. Old Mrs. Samuels says she knows how to do it. She already gave me her number and we're supposed to call when the time comes.

"You are going to the hospital where they have all them machines and such in case something goes wrong."

"It's my body and I say I'm not going." She's a feisty little pain in the ass. "If you didn't rival my cow for size I'd tan your ass for sassing me." That hand went to her hip and that finger got to wagging in my face. "Try it. Remember

what happened the last time you found yourself spanking me?"

"Yeah, you almost fucked my dick raw." Her face went red as a cherry. "Not that, I brained you with the skillet remember?" "And if I recall that got you another ass whupping." She's so cute when she gets all fired up I just wanna grab her up and kiss her until she's my soft little Angel again.

We'd been having this same argument for the past week and I aim to win it. First of all I made the biggest mistake of my life when I took her into town with me a few months ago.

Miss Friendly had to smile and talk to everybody we met. Now every time I turn around one of their meddling asses is sniffing around my place. No matter how I grumble and complain she just pats me on the head and does as she please anyhow.

I put a stop to that right quick though. I let her see just how those people really are and I ain't ashamed of it either. One day while we were picking up some butter pecan ice cream

which she's taken to eating by the gallon, I saw that little fast miss who almost undressed me in the can food aisle.

I knew damn good and well Melanie was heading back my way but when that girl got to telling me what all she wanted to do with me, I didn't stop her.

If Melanie wasn't already breeding I would've let her scalp her the way she wanted when she walked up and heard the colorful things she had planned for my dick. But all I did was grab her up and drag her back home.

Now she's not too keen on friends coming out here and we go into town maybe once a month same as I always did. She still waves and says hello but she's not on the friend seeking circuit no more.

She got on the computer one day and did her own research. I guess I shouldn't have sold her so much on the old way of doing things because now all I hear about is midwives this and midwives that. That's where we part company.

"You're being a hypocrite T." I don't care what she says her ass is going to the general hospital and having that baby.

I let her rant and rave and have her fit until she got on my damn nerves and I had to bend her over one of the stalls and fuck her quiet.

"Now go take your nap and behave." She turned up here nose at me but wobbled her ass back to the house. I was busy trying to get the place ready for when the baby came and trying not to scare myself half to death with all the stuff I was reading about birthing.

The town's people were good for one thing though. When that trollop that I'd dispatched to hell's daddy came looking for her after all this time they convinced him she'd run off with the no count pansy man she had in my bed.

Because he'd apparently forbid her to see the boy because he wasn't rich, he believed it and left me the hell alone. Not that I was

scared, hogs don't leave anything but the teeth and I got rid of those a long time ago.

She was baking bread when I went in a few hours later. I stood in the doorway and watched her kneading dough, her little round belly sticking out in front, flour on her cheeks and the heat from the oven making the hair around her face stick to her skin. I guess I was the overgrown horse's ass she was cussing to herself.

I rolled my eyes at her language and walked over to put my arms around her from behind. "I'm scared baby." She stopped and turned to look up at me. "Of what T?"

"Of something happening to you. That old lady is a hundred if she's a day I don't trust her to take care of you. I only saw where there's three people in the last year that she helped with a birthing, the hospital do that many a day."

She ran her hands up and down my chest soothingly. "There's nothing to be scared of. I talked to one of the women she delivered

and she had nothing but good things to say." I brushed the hair back from her face and looked down at her.

So much has changed since that day she thought I was sending her away. We'd gone into town and got hitched, that's what started the friend brigade come to think of it.

She had the freedom to go anywhere she liked, as long as I was with her of course, and she even knew where the kcys to the truck were. I don't think she'd driven it more than once.

I still wasn't ready to let her go into town on her own, but not because I thought she'd keep driving, but because I didn't trust anyone period. "You know I can't give you what you want right? I don't know that woman and I don't trust her to take care of you and the baby. When the time comes I'm taking you to the hospital where they can take care of you."

She went back to being spitting mad and I went back to packing her suitcase for when the baby comes which should be any day now.

She didn't say two words to me the rest of the evening but come bed time I reminded her who was boss.

If I weren't careful she'd take my balls just like half the damn men in the country. Because I like to spoil her she thinks that means she can get over on me, fat chance.

As long as there's breath in my body I'm gonna see that she's safe. I can buy her all the nonsense her little heart desires no problem, but when it comes to her care there's no question she'll do as I say.

And that's how our twins came to be born at the hospital with that damn old woman attending her, and the doctor on the sidelines just in case.

Epilogue

T-Bone

***

The springs in the old bed squeaked as I rocked back and forth inside her. The old straw mattress was barely holding up under the strain. I guess it was time for a new one at that. This one had seen us through six years of marriage and five kids with another one on the way, and that's after it had been in the family for nearly forty years.

"Fuck Angel, how come your pussy's still so sweet after all these years?" She didn't bother to answer just added a little more heat to her hips as she worked my cock but good.

Good thing the little ones were dead asleep in their rooms across the hall, because the way noise carried in this old farmhouse they would've been in for an earful.

JORDAN SILVER

It was so cold out I only hiked her nightdress up and pulled my dick through the flap of my pajama bottoms, but it got the job done, except for her tits.

I never enjoyed a good fuck without spending time on the nipple so I'd had to pop a few buttons when she got huffy. The fire was going in the grate that should keep her warm if my plowing her belly wasn't enough.

It's no secret that I'm always after my wife, hell anybody would be she's gorgeous. She's still a willful little thing, though these days a good paddling usually works to calm her ass down. That, and keeping her belly full with my babies.

No matter how she griped and moaned as soon as she dropped one and her healing period was over, I was in her ass again. Well you know what I mean. Ass fucking is for those times when the pussy is indisposed. Any other time I like the sweet warm silk of her pussy.

This morning, I woke up like every other morning, with my hand wrapped around her

pregnant belly and my dick doing what he does best, poking her in the ass. It didn't take much to lift the back of her nightdress, scoot forward some and ease right on in there.

Ahhhh, nothing like hot pussy on a cold December morning. The little ones will be up any second looking for their breakfast so I gotta make it quick.

She's pretending to be asleep but her little ass pushed back to take me all in. I'm sure she's biting into that bottom lip of hers to keep from crying out how good it is and I'm trying to keep the bed springs from making too much noise.

Our four year old twins are just about the nosiest lil somebodies you could ever find, especially Annie. She usually starts off and then drags her sister Rose along with her.

"Open your legs a little Angel." I whispered in her ear letting her know I knew darn good and well she's awake and enjoying her early morning fuck. She tried to play stubborn so I bit down on her neck and her leg

popped right up. Oh yeah, I'm in there now for sure.

"Momma..."
Well shit, Angel sped up her motions trying to cum before nosy bee came knocking. If she thinks she's leaving me high and dry hah. I turned her all the way over and pulled her up to her hands and knees, mounting her from behind. Just like the stallion covered the mare two days ago.

She'd got so hot after seeing that, same as she does every year when I take her down to the barn for a breeding. She'd let me fuck her right there in the old barn, keening and moaning all the while. Since she was already six months pregnant that one was just for the hell of it.

I sank my cock all the way in nice and slow, I don't want to hurt the child in her womb. She still loves getting fucked from behind; come to think of it she loves fucking period.

JORDAN SILVER

Meanwhile, I was plowing into Melanie hard as fuck while she bit her pillow and pushed back at me taking me all the way in.

When I came, the grunt was loud enough to shake the rafters. I shook and panted over her back as her pussy worked gymnastics on my cock, her ass still moving as she tried to get the last of my cum. Greedy ass.

She messed around and my dick hit her sweet spot and she couldn't stifle those screams. Oh well; I'll figure out what to tell my nosy ass daughter later. Right now, I got cows to milk and feed. "I'll see you later sweet Angel." I kissed her sweaty brow and hopped out of bed, ready to face the new day.

THE END

Printed in Great Britain
by Amazon